Copyright © 2016 by Mitchell Lane Publishers, Inc. All rights reserved. No part of this book may be reproduced without written permission from the publisher. Printed and bound in the United States of America.

Printing   1   2   3   4   5   6   7   8

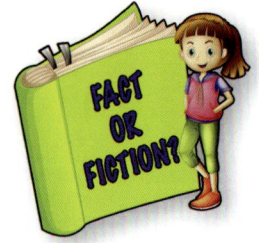

Audie Murphy
Buffalo Bill Cody
The Buffalo Soldiers
Davey Crockett

Eliot Ness
Francis Marion (Swamp Fox)
Robin Hood
Wyatt Earp

Library of Congress Cataloging-in-Publication Data
Mattern, Joanne, 1963–
 Audie Murphy / by Joanne Mattern.
    pages cm. — (Fact or fiction?)
 Includes bibliographical references and index.
 Audience: Grades 3–6.
 ISBN 978-1-61228-954-0 (library bound)
 1. Murphy, Audie, 1924–1971. 2. United States. Army—Biography—Juvenile literature. 3. World War, 1939–1945—Campaigns—Western Front—Juvenile literature. 4. Medal of honor—Biography—Juvenile literature. 5. Soldiers—United States—Biography—Juvenile literature. 6. Motion picture actors and actresses—United States—Biography—Juvenile literature. I. Title.
 U53.M87M37 2015
 940.54'1273092—dc23
 [B]
                                                                              2015003178

eBook ISBN: 978-1-61228-955-7

PBP

CONTENTS

Chapter 1
A National Hero 5

Chapter 2
Tough Times in Texas 9

Chapter 3
Audie Joins the Army 13

Chapter 4
To Hell and Back 19

Chapter 5
A Troubled Movie Star 23

Fact or Fiction? 26
Chapter Notes 28
Glossary 30
Works Consulted 31
Further Reading 31
On the Internet 31
Index 32

Words in **bold** throughout can be found in the Glossary.

Because of his heroic actions in World War II, Audie Murphy became the most decorated soldier in US history. But this young farm boy paid a terrible price for his wartime experiences.

CHAPTER 1

A National Hero

June 2, 1945, was a sunny day at an airfield near Salzburg, Austria. During World War II, the airfield had been abuzz with German warplanes taking off and landing. However, the war in Europe had ended just a few weeks earlier. Today, the airfield was busy for another reason. The United States was about to honor one of its greatest wartime heroes with the Medal of Honor, the highest US **military** award. In recognition of its importance, nine US senators had made the long flight to Austria to attend the ceremony. They joined thousands of his fellow soldiers, who stood at attention.

The hero was not quite twenty years old, and he looked even younger. Lieutenant General Alexander Patch stepped forward to present the medal and saw tears in the young soldier's eyes. "Are you nervous?" Patch asked. "Yes, sir, I'm afraid I am,"[1] the soldier replied.

He also received the Legion of Merit. This award recognized any member of the US armed forces who performed outstanding services. In total, during and after the war, that young soldier received a record

Chapter 1

thirty-seven medals. Eleven of those medals were for **valor**, or bravery.[2]

Who was this soldier, who had done so many incredible deeds while still in his teens? His name was Audie Murphy, and he was the most **decorated** American **combat** soldier in World War II. Murphy rose from a lowly **infantry** soldier to an officer whose bravery captured the hearts of the American people. During his two years at war, Murphy reportedly killed 240 enemy soldiers, more than any other soldier.

After he returned home, Audie's incredible story and good looks caught the attention of Hollywood. Audie went on to appear in a number of movies, including one based on his own wartime experiences. These movies added to Audie's legend as a fearless soldier who would stop at nothing to help his fellow soldiers and preserve his country's honor.

Audie Murphy remained a household name and a symbol of battlefield bravery until his death in 1971. However, his image of a tough, ruthless killing machine was far from the truth. Audie did not enjoy killing others, and he did not really care about all the medals and honors he received. After seeing several close friends and many of his fellow soldiers killed in combat, Audie believed that "the real heroes were the ones with the wooden crosses,"[3] meaning the ones who had died. He also stated, "I never liked being called the 'most decorated' soldier. There were so many guys who should have gotten medals and never did—guys who were killed."[4]

In 1971, a Veterans of Foreign Wars post in Virginia erected this monument near the site of the plane crash that killed Audie. Because Audie lied about his birthdate so he could join the Army, the year listed on this monument and on Audie's grave is incorrect.

Fighting in World War II affected Murphy deeply and made the remaining years of his life difficult and often unhappy. While there is no denying the brave things he did and the lives he saved, the truth about Murphy and his experiences during World War II is not what many people believe. What is fact and what is fiction about this American hero? Let's find out.

Thousands of poor sharecroppers lived in rough shacks like this one in Texas during the first half of the 20th century. These houses had no running water, electricity, or indoor plumbing and provided only the most basic shelter from the weather.

CHAPTER 2

Tough Times in Texas

Audie Leon Murphy was born on June 20, 1925,[1] in a tiny shack in a cotton field near the town of Kingston, Texas. Audie's parents, Emmett and Josie Murphy, were **sharecroppers**. They picked cotton in fields owned by someone else. In exchange for their work, they were given a shabby house to live in and a tiny share of the money they earned. Like other tenant farmers' homes, the Murphy house had no electricity, running water, or bathrooms.

The Murphy family would eventually include twelve children, nine of whom lived to adulthood. The family was desperately poor, and both parents had to work in the cotton fields. Audie's mother could not afford to take any time off after having a baby. Josie Murphy strapped him into a baby swing while she picked cotton. By the time Audie and his brothers and sisters were four or five years old, they were in the fields, picking cotton alongside their parents.

Emmett Murphy was not the hardest-working man in Texas. He much preferred to play dominoes or gamble than work. Many of his neighbors complained that if they hired Murphy to do a job,

Children as young as this four-year-old boy joined their parents and other family members in the fields. They were expected to work as hard as their parents did and had little time for school or play.

they had to stand over him and watch him to make sure the job got done.[2] Audie Murphy did not think much of his father or the fact that he and Josie had more children than they could provide for. He later said, "Every time my old man couldn't feed the kids he had, he got him another one."[3] After the war, Audie wrote that his father "was not lazy, but he had a genius for not considering the future."[4]

Audie's childhood was filled with hard work and crushing poverty. The family moved several times.

Tough Times in Texas

Usually they lived in tiny, falling-down shacks. A few times, they even lived in a railroad boxcar. There was little to eat. Most meals consisted of cornbread, gravy, and molasses. The only meat the family enjoyed came from small animals such as rabbits, squirrels, and birds that Audie and his brothers killed with their hunting rifles. In 1956, Audie compared his childhood to war. "People know me for my record as a soldier. But the truth is I must have done some of my best fighting in a war I was in long before I joined the Army. You might say there never was a 'peace time' in my life, a time when things were good. . . . I never had just 'fun.'. . . I never had time to play. . . . I never had a bike. It was a full-time job just existing."[5]

When Audie was about nine, his family moved to the small town of Celeste, Texas. Many people in town did not like the Murphys. Emmett Murphy drifted from job to job and did not pay the monthly rent on his tiny house. His children did not have enough to eat and wore shabby clothes. As most of the children got older, they seemed to be as lazy as their father. Neighbors had nothing good to say about the family—except for Audie.

Audie was different from the rest of his family. He was a good student in school and loved to read. He would go into Celeste's tiny drugstore and read every magazine he could find. He was eager to work and determined to do something with his life. Still, it seemed that Audie was nothing more than a poor Texas boy with no future.

Audie Murphy joined the US Army when he was just seventeen years old. It was his only escape from a life of crushing poverty.

CHAPTER 3

Audie Joins the Army

When Audie became a teenager, life got even harder. His father left, never to return. It was up to Audie to support his family. He quit school and went to work. He also helped feed the family by hunting. Audie became an amazingly good shot. A neighbor once loaned Audie his rifle with eight bullets in it. When Audie came home, he was carrying four dead rabbits—and there were still four bullets left in the gun.[1] This "training" would serve him well a few years later when he joined the army.

Audie Murphy was angry when his father left the family. However, his mother was heartbroken. Josie Murphy still had three young children at home, and she was unable to take care of them on her own. She went to live with her daughter, Corinne, and Corinne's family in a nearby town. Meanwhile, Audie moved in with a local family and earned money by working on their farm.

Audie adored his mother. It was hard for him to watch her struggle after his father left. Josie's health had never been that good, and now she began to fail quickly. On May 23, 1941, Josie Murphy died of **pneumonia** and a heart condition. She was forty-nine

Chapter 3

years old. Audie put part of the blame on his father. He later wrote, "Her story, including her early death, is not unusual in the history of a sharecropper's family, particularly when the sharecropper himself runs off, leaving his wife to take care of their children."[2]

There was no way sixteen-year-old Audie could take care of his younger sisters and brother, so they were sent to an orphanage. Audie went back to work at a series of low-paying jobs. Farm work paid about a dollar a day. Later he worked in a grocery store and made twelve dollars a week.[3] Since Audie only had a fifth-grade education, it seemed impossible that he would ever rise above his poor life and achieve his dream of becoming better than his father was.

Then, on December 7, 1941, the Japanese Navy attacked American army and navy bases at Pearl Harbor in Hawaii, and everything changed. World War II had started on September 1, 1939. However, the United States had stayed out of the fighting—until now. With their country suddenly at war, young men were lining up to join the armed forces and fight.

Audie wanted to do the same thing. There was just one problem: He was too young. He was also very small—just five feet, five inches tall and 110 pounds—which made him look even younger. His efforts to enlist failed. Audie's sister, Corinne, helped him get a false birth certificate, which showed his birth year as 1924 rather than 1925. So ten days after his "eighteenth" birthday (in reality he was seventeen), Audie was accepted into the infantry.

Audie Joins the Army

Audie underwent basic training in Texas. His commanders were worried about Audie's youth and small size. They tried to transfer him to a school for cooks and bakers, but Audie refused to go. He wanted to be a fighting soldier. Later, he went to Fort Meade in Maryland for further training. In February, 1943, Audie was shipped to Casablanca in North Africa for still more training. A few months later, he was ready to fight.

Audie was assigned to Company B, 1st **Battalion**, 15th Infantry Regiment of the 3rd Infantry Division and landed on the Italian island of Sicily, where he killed his first enemy soldiers. It didn't take long before Audie realized that war was not an adventure at all. It was hard, heartbreaking, and bloody work. "I have seen war as it actually is, and I do not like it. But I will go on fighting,"[4] he later wrote in his autobiography, *To Hell and Back*.

Audie's division soon crossed over to the Italian mainland. One day, Audie, now a **sergeant**, and his men were pinned down in a house with German tanks coming closer and closer. Audie radioed the tanks' position to American warships just offshore. Gunfire from the ships destroyed the first tank, blocking the road and keeping Audie and his men safe. During the night, Audie heard the Germans repairing the tank. Realizing the danger, he led his men in an **ambush** to blow up the tank and kill the enemy soldiers.

In August 1944, the 3rd Division landed in southern France. By then, Audie had already seen

Audie Murphy poses for a picture in his US Army uniform in June 1945, just a few weeks after the war in Europe ended with the defeat of Nazi Germany.

Audie Joins the Army

> RÉPUBLIQUE FRANÇAISE
>
> EXTRAIT DU DECRET EN DATE DU 19 JUILLET 1948
> Portant nomination dans la Légion d'Honneur
>
> Article 1er - Sont nommés dans l'Ordre National de la Légion d'Honneur
> AU GRADE DE CHEVALIER
>
> "Pour services exceptionnels de guerre rendus au cours des opérations de libération de la France".
>
> MURPHY Audie L. - Lieutenant - Armée Américaine -
>
> "Magnifique combattant qui, après s'être distingué en Sicile à Palerme et à Auzio, a pris une part glorieuse aux batailles menées pour la Libération de la France".
>
> "Débarqué le 15 août à Ramatuelle avec la 3ème Division d'Infanterie Américaine, a fait preuve en toutes circonstances et en particulier lors de la bataille de Colmar où sa division combattait dans les rangs de la 1ère Armée Française, d'un héroïsme exceptionnel".
>
> CES NOMINATIONS COMPORTENT L'ATTRIBUTION DE LA CROIX DE GUERRE 1939-1945 AVEC PALME.
>
> Fait à Paris, le 19 juillet 1948
> Par le Président de la République   Vincent AURIOL
> Le Secrétaire d'Etat aux Forces Armées (Guerre)
> Max LEJEUNE
>
> Le Ministre des Forces Armées
> PH TEITGEN
>
> Le Ministre des Affaires Etrangères
> Georges BIDAULT
>
> Le Président du Conseil des Ministres
> SCHUMAN
>
> EXTRAIT CERTIFIE CONFORME
> PARIS, le 1 AOUT 1979
> Le Chef du Bureau des Décorations
> PO/L'Adjoint au Chef de la Section "Décorations Diverses"
>
> René LABRO

The French government awarded its "Au Grade de Chevalier" award to Audie for his accomplishments during the war to free France from control by the Germans.

many soldiers in his battalion killed, and he had done his share of killing. He was known as a fearless soldier who could think on his feet, and he was well-liked by the other soldiers and his commanding officers. The stage was set for the most heroic actions of Audie's life—actions that would make him famous around the world.

Audie shakes hands with French General Jean de Lattre de Tassigny after receiving France's Legion of Merit award for his heroic actions in battle during World War II.

CHAPTER 4

To Hell and Back

Audie's best friend in the army was Lattie Tipton. Audie and Lattie had been through a lot together, fighting, surviving, and seeing their friends killed and wounded. Soon after the landing, they were ordered to attack a hill topped with a large German **pillbox**, armed with a cannon. Several machine gun nests lower on the hill protected the pillbox. Covered by his fellow soldiers, Audie advanced up the hill by himself in the teeth of heavy German fire and killed a number of the enemy. He came back down to re-arm, then headed back up again.

Audie thought he was alone, but realized that Lattie was beside him. Together they moved up the hill, killing every enemy soldier they found. Finally, the Germans manning one of the machine guns held up a white flag, which showed they wanted to **surrender**.

Lattie started to get up to accept the surrender, but Audie was suspicious. He yelled at Lattie to get down, but his friend didn't listen. As soon as he stood up, the Germans fired at him. Lattie was killed instantly.

Chapter 4

Audie was stunned. For a moment, he lay near his dead friend. Then he pulled out a **grenade** and threw it at the German position, killing the machine gunners. At that moment, something changed in Audie. He later wrote, "I remember the experience as I do a nightmare. A demon seems to have entered my body. My brain is coldly alert and logical. I do not think of the danger to myself. My whole being is concentrated on killing."[1] Audie grabbed the German machine gun and advanced up the hill, firing it from his hip and killing every German soldier before the rest of his battalion was able to join him.

His actions that day won Audie the Distinguished Service Cross, the army's second-highest decoration. He kept on fighting, as if being active all the time could stop him from thinking too much.

Less than two months later, he won the Silver Star, the third-highest medal a solider can receive. He followed a group of officers inspecting the front lines in a wooded area. German soldiers opened fire on the group, trapping them in a shallow hole. Before the Germans could kill them, Audie ran up and threw several grenades. When the smoke cleared, all the German soldiers were dead or wounded and the Americans were safe. Three days later he won a second Silver Star, and a week afterward received a battlefield promotion to **second lieutenant**.

Audie had always managed to escape battles without serious injuries, but his luck ran out on October 26, 1944, when he was shot in the hip. The wound got infected, and Audie spent more than two months in a hospital. He rejoined his unit in January 1945. A few days later, the Americans were attacked near the village of Hiltzwihr by a strong German force of tanks and hundreds of infantrymen. As the Germans threatened to overrun the American position, Audie ordered his men to retreat to safety. He leaped onto a burning US **tank destroyer** and began firing its machine gun. He cut down so many German soldiers—some of whom got within ten yards (nine meters) of him—that the tanks were forced to retreat. Audie hopped down and rejoined his men. Moments later, the tank destroyer exploded. Audie earned the Medal of Honor for his heroics during this action.

By the time the war in Europe ended in May 1945, Audie's bravery and battlefield actions were known around the world. When he returned home, he was given parades and greeted as a hero. He even appeared on the cover of *Life* magazine, one of the most important magazines of its time.

However, Audie did not feel like a hero inside. He told interviewers that, far from being fearless, he was very much afraid. "I was scared before every battle,"[2] he admitted. What kept him fighting was his love for the men he fought with. "Loyalty to your **comrades**, when you come right down to it, has more to do with bravery in battle than even **patriotism** does. You may want to be brave, but your spirit can desert you when things really get rough. Only you find you can't let your comrades down and in the pinch they can't let you down either."[3]

After his return home, Audie starred in many Hollywood Westerns. Here he appears as Captain Bruce Coburn in *40 Guns to Apache Pass,* which was released in 1967. Audie grew tired of filming Westerns, complaining that the characters and the plots were always the same.

CHAPTER 5

A Troubled Movie Star

After Audie returned to Texas, a new adventure awaited him. A famous actor named Jimmy Cagney had seen Audie's picture on the cover of *Life* magazine and thought he should be an actor. Cagney invited Audie to come to Hollywood. Audie lived with Cagney for over a year, but his acting career did not go far. Audie ended up sleeping at a gym owned by his friend, Terry Hunt. Over the next few years, Audie got a few small roles in movies. In 1949, he published *To Hell and Back*, a book about his war experiences.

When the Korean War broke out in 1950, Audie joined the Texas National Guard and thought about going back into combat. However, his personal life changed his plans. Audie had married an actress named Wanda Hendrix in 1949, but the marriage only lasted fifteen months. In 1951, Audie married Pamela Archer. The couple had two sons. Audie did not want to leave his family to go to war. He also knew that making movies was the best way to support his wife and children. Audie made a few Westerns, but he was poorly paid and felt like every movie was the same as the one before. "The faces are the same,

Chapter 5

and so is the dialogue. Only horses are changed,"[1] he once said about acting in Westerns.

In 1951, Audie starred in the movie *The Red Badge of Courage*, based on the famous book about a soldier during the Civil War. Audie was perfect for the part of the soldier Henry Fleming. Like Audie, Fleming came face-to-face with the horrors of war and overcame his fear to become a brave soldier. However, the movie did not do well at the box office.

Audie's book, *To Hell and Back*, had been a bestseller and Universal Studios decided to make it into a movie. Audie was asked to star, but at first he refused. He did not want the public to think he was trying to become more famous by playing up his position as a war hero. He changed his mind because he wanted to show the bravery of all the soldiers who had fought and died. Audie was also closely involved with the production. He made sure the equipment was painted the right colors, the uniforms were correct, and every detail of the battles was as true as possible.[2]

The movie came out in 1955 and was a huge hit. It was Universal Studio's highest earning movie until 1975[3] and the high point of Audie's acting career. Audie went on to appear in forty-four movies and three television productions over the course of his career.[4]

Although Audie was a hero onscreen, real life was difficult for him. His war experiences never left him in peace. Audie had trouble sleeping and he

A Troubled Movie Star

jumped with fear whenever he heard a loud noise. He slept with the lights on and a gun under his pillow.

Today, Audie's problem is called **post-traumatic stress disorder**, but that term did not exist during the 1950s and 1960s. "To be trained to kill, and then to come back into civilian life and be alone in the crowd—it takes an awful long time to get over it. Fear and depression come over you,"[5] Audie told journalist Thomas Morgan in 1967. During the last years of his life, Audie spoke out about his experiences so the government and the public would better understand the problems returning soldiers faced.

Audie Murphy was killed in a plane crash on May 28, 1971. He was forty-five years old. He was buried at Arlington National Cemetery with full military honors. However, Audie had asked that his gravestone be plain and not decorated with the gold trim to which he was entitled as a Medal of Honor winner.[6] Although he was America's most decorated and famous soldier, Audie Murphy really didn't want to be remembered as a war hero. He may not have been successful in this regard. After President John F. Kennedy, Audie's gravesite is the second-most-visited at Arlington.

FACT OR FICTION?

There is no doubt that Audie Murphy was a brave soldier who would do anything for his men in combat. However, not everything about Audie's life and experiences is as wonderful as they seem to be.

Audie was a hero in many ways. He dragged himself out of poverty to become a famous actor and role model. His actions during war saved the lives of many of the men in his division.

However, being a war hero is not as easy in real life as it is in books or the movies. It also wasn't easy to live up to the things America wanted to believe about its war heroes. Soon after Audie returned to Texas after the war, he was interviewed by Associated Press reporter William Barnard. Audie told Barnard how being home made him feel peaceful. "Here I am riding along a highway—but I'm not watching every bit of the way for mines. . . . All this makes me feel fine,"[1] he said.

Audie's words were what Americans wanted to hear. Everyone was happy that the war was over and family members were back home. Surely the soldiers could get back to their normal lives, as if nothing had

The truth was, Audie was not fine, nor were many others. Like many soldiers, Audie missed the excitement and danger of combat. He later wrote, "War robs you mentally and physically, it drains you. Things don't thrill you anymore. It's a struggle everyday to find something interesting to do."[2] Years later, Audie spoke more about how war had changed him. "War is like a giant pack rat, it takes something from you and it leaves something behind in its stead. It burned me out in some ways so that now I feel like an old man but still sometimes act like a dumb kid. It made me grow up too fast. You live so much on nervous excitement that when it is over you fall apart."[3]

Audie's image was also affected by the movie *To Hell and Back*. In his book, Audie is honest about the horror of war. However, the movie version of his story was much less bloody and not as honest about the reality of combat. Audie was not completely happy about the movie and the way it showed war. He called it "a Western in uniform."[4] Along with being much less **graphic** than his book, the movie changed a number of little details. The real battles in Italy and France were muddy, wet, and cold. However, in the movie, major battle scenes were shot on sunny days.[5] Changing these details might not seem important, but it gave viewers a false idea that war wasn't really so terrible.

Audie Murphy ended *To Hell and Back*, by saying "I may be branded by war, but I will not be defeated by it."[6] Audie was not defeated by war, but his combat experiences hurt him in ways that could never fully heal. Though Audie Murphy was a hero, being a hero isn't always as glorious and exciting as people like to believe.

CHAPTER NOTES

Chapter 1: A National Hero
1. Don Graham, *No Name on the Bullet: A Biography of Audie Murphy* (New York: Viking, 1989), p. 101.
2. Ibid.
3. Audie Murphy, *To Hell and Back* (New York: Holt, Rinehart, and Winston, 1949), p. 6.
4. Graham, p. vii.

Chapter 2: Tough Times in Texas
1. "Audie L. Murphy Memorial Website," http://audiemurphy.com/biography.htm
2. Don Graham, *No Name on the Bullet: A Biography of Audie Murphy* (New York: Viking, 1989), p. 6.
3. *Biography: Audie Murphy: Great American Hero.* A&E Television Networks, 1996.
4. Graham, p. 6.
5. Ibid., p. 8.

Chapter 3: Audie Joins the Army
1. Don Graham, *No Name on the Bullet: A Biography of Audie Murphy* (New York: Viking, 1989), p. 16.
2. Ibid., p.19.
3. Ibid., p.20.
4. Audie Murphy, *To Hell and Back* (New York: Holt, Rinehart, and Winston, 1949), p. 15.

Chapter 4: To Hell and Back
1. Audie Murphy, *To Hell and Back* (New York: Holt, Rinehart, and Winston, 1949), p.175.
2. "Quotes of Audie Murphy." http://www.audiemurphy.com/documents/doc050/QuotesOfAudieMurphy.pdf
3. Ibid.

CHAPTER NOTES

Chapter 5: A Troubled Movie Star
1. "Quotes of Audie Murphy." http://www.audiemurphy.com/documents/doc050/QuotesOfAudieMurphy.pdf
2. Rob Nixon, "Articles: To Hell and Back (1955)." TCM.com. http://www.tcm.com/tcmdb/title/93456/To-Hell-and_Back/articles.html
3. "Audie Murphy." Biography.com. http://www.biography.com/people/audie-murphy-9418662
4. Sue Gossett, *The Films and Career of Audie Murphy, America's Real Hero* (Madison, NC: Empire Publishing, 1996), pp. 5-6.
5. Tom Huntington. "Audie Murphy: A Life Larger Than Legend." America in WWII. http://www.americaninwwii.com/articles/audie-murphy-a-life-larger-than-legend/
6. Rob Nixon, "Articles: To Hell and Back (1955)."

Fact or Fiction?
1. Don Graham, *No Name on the Bullet: A Biography of Audie Murphy* (New York: Viking, 1989), p.106.
2. "Quotes of Audie Murphy." http://www.audiemurphy.com/documents/doc050/QuotesOfAudieMurphy.pdf
3. Ibid.
4. Rob Nixon, "Articles: To Hell and Back (1955)." TCM.com. http://www.tcm.com/tcmdb/title/93456/To-Hell-and_Back/articles.html
5. Ibid.
6. Audie Murphy, *To Hell and Back* (New York: Holt, Rinehart, and Winston, 1949), p. 273.

GLOSSARY

ambush (AM-bush)—a sudden, surprise attack

battalion (buh-TAL-yuhn)—a body of soldiers, ranging between four hundred and one thousand men

combat (KAHM-bat)—fighting during wartime

comrades (KOM-radz)—companions; fellow soldiers

decorated (DEH-kuh-ray-tuhd)—awarded medals or honors

graphic (GRAF-ik)—shown or described in a very clear way

grenade (gruh-NADE)—a small explosive device thrown by hand

infantry (IN-fan-tree)—soldiers who fight on foot

military (MIL-uh-tare-ee)—having to do with soldiers or the armed forces

patriotism (PAY-tree-uh-tiz-uhm)—loyalty and love for one's country

pillbox (PILL-box)—a small concrete fortification with openings for weapons to fire

pneumonia (noo-MONE-yuh)—an infection of the lungs

post-traumatic stress disorder (POST traw-MAT-ik STRESS diss-OHR-duhr)—a condition of emotional stress that occurs as a result of injury or shock

second lieutenant (loo-TEN-uhnt)—the lowest-ranking commissioned officer in the US Army

sergeant (SAHR-juhnt)—a non-commissioned officer in the armed forces

sharecroppers (SHARE-crop-urz)—people who farm someone else's land in exchange for a house and a small percentage of the money earned from the sale of crops

surrender (sur-REN-duhr)—to give up to an enemy

tank destroyer (TANK deh-STROI-uhr)—armored vehicle designed specifically to attack enemy tanks

valor (VAL-or)—bravery

PHOTO CREDITS: All design elements from Thinkstock/Sharon Beck. Cover, pp. 1, 23—ZUMA Archive/ZUMAPRESS/Newscom; cover (background), pp. 1 (background), 3, 5, 9, 13, 19, 23, 26–27—Thinkstock; p. 4—US Army; p. 7—Jwalden/cc-by-sa; pp. 8, 10—Library of Congress; pp. 12, 16, 18—Everett Collection/Newscom; p. 17—US National Archives and Records Administration; p. 25—Tim1965/cc-by-sa.

WORKS CONSULTED

"Audie Murphy." Biography.com. http://www.biography.com/people/audie-murphy-9418662

"Audie L. Murphy Memorial Website." http://www.audiemurphy.com

Biography: Audie Murphy: Great American Hero. A&E Television Networks, 1996.

Gossett, Sue. *The Films and Career of Audie Murphy, America's Real Hero.* Madison, NC: Empire Publishing, 1996.

Graham, Don. *No Name on the Bullet: A Biography of Audie Murphy.* New York: Viking, 1989.

Huntington, Tom. "Audie Murphy: A Life Larger Than Legend." *America in WWII*, February, 2007. http://www.americaninwwii.com/articles/audie-murphy-a-life-larger-than-legend/

Murphy, Audie. *To Hell and Back.* New York: Holt, Rinehart, and Winston, 1949.

Nixon, Rob. "Articles: To Hell and Back (1955)." TCM.com. http://www.tcm.com/tcmdb/title/93456/To-Hell-and_Back/articles.html

To Hell and Back. Universal International Pictures, 1955.

"To Hell and Back: Full Synopsis." TCM.com. http://www.tcm.com/tcmdb/title/93456/To-Hell-and_Back/full-synopsis.html

FURTHER READING

Alter, Dr. Judy. *Audie Murphy: War Hero and Movie Star.* Austin, TX: State House Press, 2007.

Callery, Sean. *World War II.* New York: Scholastic, 2013.

Caravantes, Peggy. *American Hero: The Audie Murphy Story.* Greensboro, NC: Avisson Press, 2004.

Wachtel, Roger. *The Medal of Honor.* Brookfield, CT: Children's Press, 2009.

ON THE INTERNET

"Audie L. Murphy Memorial Website." http://www.audiemurphy.com

———. "The Amazing Life of Audie Murphy." *Mental Floss*, August 20, 2009. http://mentalfloss.com/article/22570/amazing-life-audie-murphy

INDEX

Archer, Pamela 23
Arlington National Cemetery 25
Associated Press 26
Austria 5
Barnard, William 26
Cagney, Jimmy 23
Casablanca 15
Civil War 24
Distinguished Service Cross 20
Fleming, Henry 24
Fort Meade 15
France 15
Hendrix, Wanda 23
Hollywood 23
Hunt, Terry 23
Italy 15
Kennedy, John F. (President) 25
Korean War 23
Legion of Merit 5
Life magazine 21
Medal of Honor 5, 21, 25
Morgan, Thomas 25
Murphy, Audie Leon
   birth of 9
   family of 9–11, 14
   childhood of 10–11
   loss of father and 13–14
   death of mother and 13–14
   joins the army 14
   first war battle of 15
   heroic actions by 15, 17, 19–21
   wins Distinguished Service Cross 20
   awarded Silver Star 20
   injured in battle 20–21
   receives Medal of Honor 5, 21
   receives Legion of Merit 5
   marriages of 23
   children of 23
   film career of 23–24
   writes *To Hell and Back* 23
   and movie *To Hell and Back* 24, 27
   death of 25
   grave of 25
Murphy, Corinne 13, 14
Murphy, Emmett 9–10, 11, 13–14
Murphy, Josie 9, 10, 13–14
North Africa 15
Patch, Alexander (Lieutenant General) 5
Pearl Harbor 14
post-traumatic stress disorder 25
Red Badge of Courage, The 24
sharecroppers 9
Sicily 15
Silver Star 20
Texas 9, 11, 14, 23, 26
Texas National Guard 23
Tipton, Lattie 19–20
To Hell and Back (book) 15, 23, 24, 27
To Hell and Back (movie) 24, 27
Universal Studios 24
Westerns 23–24, 27
World War II 6, 7, 14, 15–21, 26

ABOUT THE AUTHOR

Joanne Mattern is the author of many books for children on a variety of subjects, including history and biography. She has written many biographies for Mitchell Lane. Joanne loves to learn about people, places, and events and bring historical figures to life for youthful readers. She lives in New York State with her husband, children, and several pets.